Brer Rabbit
and the Well

A Native American tale
told by Malachy Doyle

Illustrated by Mike Phillips

W
FRANKLIN WATTS

First published in 2010 by
Franklin Watts
338 Euston Road
London
NW1 3BH

Franklin Watts Australia
Level 17/207 Kent Street
Sydney
NSW 2000

Text © Malachy Doyle 2010
Illustration © Mike Phillips 2010

A CIP catalogue record for this book is available
from the British Library.

ISBN 978 0 7496 9417 3 (hbk)
ISBN 978 0 7496 9423 4 (pbk)

Series Editor: Jackie Hamley
Editor: Melanie Palmer
Series Advisor: Catherine Glavina
Series Designer: Peter Scoulding

Printed in China

To find out more about Malachy
Doyle and his books, please visit:
www.malachydoyle.com

Franklin Watts is a division of
Hachette Children's Books,
an Hachette UK company.
www.hachette.co.uk

This tale comes from North America. Can you find this on a map?

"It's time to plant some
lettuce!" said Bear.

Brer Fox and Brer Rabbit agreed and set to work.

5

They dug and they raked.

Brer Rabbit soon felt tired.

"I've a thorn in my paw,"
he groaned. "I'll go and
get a needle to pull it out."

But there was no thorn, really. Brer Rabbit just wanted a rest.

Brer Rabbit saw a bucket, hanging over a well.

"This is a good place to rest," he said, climbing in.

But Rabbit was too heavy, and the bucket fell to the bottom! WHOOSH!

"What was that?"
asked Bear.

"That's Rabbit up to his tricks again," said Brer Fox. "Rabbit! Rabbit! Where are you?"

Brer Rabbit heard him. "Here's my chance to get out," he thought. "And play a trick on that greedy Fox, too."

19

"I'm eating lots of food, Fox!" he cried. "Come down and join me!"

So Fox got into the
second bucket and it
dropped to the bottom.

But as it did, it made
Rabbit's bucket rise back
up to the top.

Rabbit jumped out.

Now Fox was stuck!

"That's what you get for being greedy, Fox!" he laughed.

Then off Brer Rabbit
hopped to see if he could
find Fox's lunch to eat.

Puzzle 1

Put these pictures in the correct order.
Now tell the story in your own words.
What different endings can you think of?

Puzzle 2

lazy   helpful
cunning

puzzled   mean
hard-working

bored   curious
cross

Choose the correct words for each character. Which words are incorrect? Turn over to find the answers.

Answers

Puzzle 1

The correct order is 1c, 2b, 3a, 4f, 5d, 6e

Puzzle 2

Brer Rabbit: the correct words are cunning, lazy

The incorrect word is helpful

Bear: the correct words are hard-working, puzzled

The incorrect word is mean

Fox: the correct words are cross, curious

The incorrect word is bored

Look out for more Leapfrog World Tales:

Chief Five Heads
ISBN 978 0 7496 8593 5*
ISBN 978 0 7496 8599 7

Baba Yaga
ISBN 978 0 7496 8594 2*
ISBN 978 0 7496 8600 0

Issun Boshi
ISBN 978 0 7496 8595 9*
ISBN 978 0 7496 8601 7

The Frog Emperor
ISBN 978 0 7496 8596 6*
ISBN 978 0 7496 8602 4

The Gold-Giving Snake
ISBN 978 0 7496 8597 3*
ISBN 978 0 7496 8603 1

The Bone Giant
ISBN 978 0 7496 8598 0*
ISBN 978 0 7496 8604 8

Bluebird and Coyote
ISBN 978 0 7496 9415 9*
ISBN 978 0 7496 9421 0

Anansi the Banana Thief
ISBN 978 0 7496 9416 6*
ISBN 978 0 7496 9422 7

Brer Rabbit and the Well
ISBN 978 0 7496 9417 3*
ISBN 978 0 7496 9423 4

Little Tiger and the Fire
ISBN 978 0 7496 9418 0*
ISBN 978 0 7496 9424 1

No Turtle Stew Today
ISBN 978 0 7496 9419 7*
ISBN 978 0 7496 9425 8

Too Many Webs for Anansi
ISBN 978 0 7496 9420 3*
ISBN 978 0 7496 9426 5

*hardback

For more Leapfrog books go to: www.franklinwatts.co.uk